A · COUNTRY · CHILDHOOD

WAR BOY

· MICHAEL · FOREMAN ·

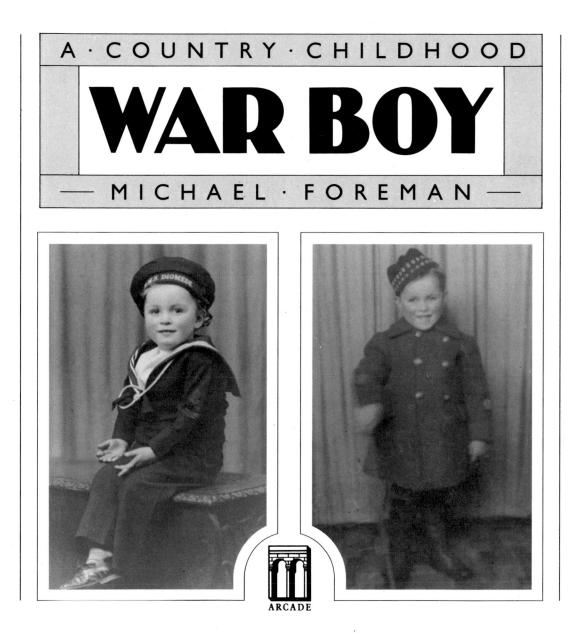

ARCADE

TO MY BROTHERS AND OUR MUM

First U.S. Edition 1990

ISBN 1-55970-049-1

Library of Congress Cataloging-in-Publication information is available.

Published in the United States by Arcade Publishing, Inc., New York, a Little, Brown company

10 9 8 7 6 5 4 3 2 1

PRINTED IN ITALY

I woke up when the bomb came through the roof.
It came through at an angle, overflew my bed by
inches, bounced up over my mother's bed, hit the
mirror, dropped into the grate and exploded up the
chimney. It was an incendiary. A fire-bomb.

My brother Ivan appeared in pyjamas and his Home Guard tin hat. Being in the Home Guard, he had ensured that all the rooms in our house were stuffed with sandbags. Ivan threw sand over the bomb but the dry sand kept sliding off. He threw the hearthrug over the bomb and jumped up and down on it, until brother Pud arrived with a bucket of wet sand from the yard. This did the trick.

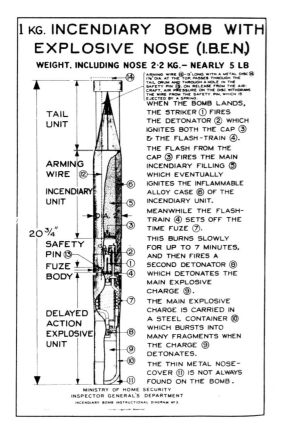

If you had collected enough cigarette cards you knew what to do.

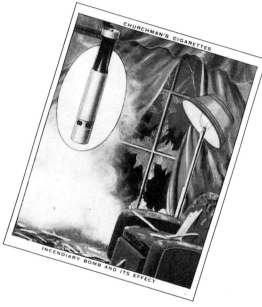

Mother grabbed me from the bed. The night sky was
filled with lights. Searchlights, anti-aircraft fire, stars and a
bombers' moon. The sky bounced as my mother ran. Just
as we reached our dug-out across the street, the sky
flared red as the church exploded.

It was Monday, April 21 1941, just before 10 p.m.
Thousands of incendiaries were dropped on our village,
Pakefield, and the neighbouring big town, Lowestoft.
The Germans were trying to set alight the thatched roof
of the church to make a beacon for the following waves
of bombers. Within a few minutes more than forty fires
were blazing in Pakefield and the southern part of
Lowestoft. Two incendiaries buried themselves in the
roof of the church. The Rector climbed ladders to
extinguish one, but was unable to reach the other.

The high explosive bombs followed immediately. More
were dropped in this raid than in any other, but with the
church now blazing, a thick mist rolled up from the sea
and ruined the bombers' night. The following waves of
bombers turned back.

We were safe. And we were together. We were three brothers and Mum. Ivan, Bernard (known to us only as Pud) and myself. (Our father had died one month before I was born.) Also with us was Aunt Louie.

In the morning we returned home. Mum went to the loo, which was outside in the yard, and found a hole in the roof and a bomb, unexploded, in the floor. Pud pulled it out and carried it to 'Pal' the policeman in the police box on the corner.

'Young Bernard!!'

My big brother Ivan worked in a garage. Brother Pud went to school every day in a nearby village, as the local school was full of soldiers.

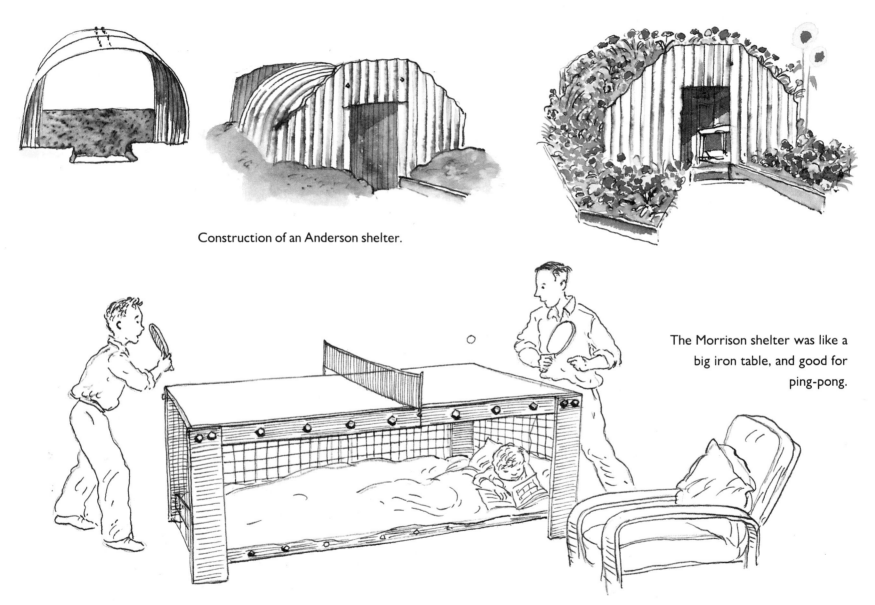

Construction of an Anderson shelter.

The Morrison shelter was like a big iron table, and good for ping-pong.

15

'Children's Corner'. No child set foot on the beach for
the duration of the war.

THE FRONT LINE

Lowestoft was a front line target throughout the war because it was a very large naval base and headquarters to the Minesweeping Service. It was Britain's nearest town to Germany, and after the fall of Holland the Germans had airfields only ninety miles away. Lowestoft and the surrounding area became a practice ground for the Luftwaffe, just a twenty-minute hop to the virtually defenceless coast.

Britain's defences were concentrated around Dover and the Channel ports. When France fell in 1940, Lowestoft did not have a single gun. Fake guns were installed. The first real guns to arrive were two 1917 field guns with wooden wheels. The very young gun crews lived in holiday beach huts.

The sea defences, scaffold poles and barbed wire, stretched as far as the eye could see along the beach. Mines were hidden in the sand. Concrete blockhouses or pillboxes squatted along the cliff-top.

At Pakefield we had a massive gun emplacement with a fake gun – three scaffold poles strapped together and covered with camouflage netting. (The netting mysteriously disappeared one night and suddenly Bumshie Fuller had a strangely coloured shrimp trawl net.)

Further along the cliff at the old Pakefield holiday camp were more gun emplacements which eventually had real guns, but initially were just piles of fish-boxes filled with sand. More real guns were on the cliff next to the Palais de Dance and the Grand Hotel (which served as the Czech Army Headquarters).

Lowestoft was ringed with anti-tank blocks and deep ditches called tank traps which rapidly filled with water. (Brother Pud and friends caught sticklebacks and newts in Easy's pond and stocked up all the tank traps. Thereafter the local boys had a multitude of fishing places in addition to the two or three traditional ponds.)

Pillboxes lurked in hedgerows and at cross-roads. Some pillboxes were disguised as haystacks and stood about innocently beside country roads. Others along the coast pretended to be holiday chalets or ice-cream stalls.

At the beginning of the Black Out there were more casualties from road accidents than from enemy actions. White lines were painted along kerbs and men were encouraged to leave their white shirt tails hanging out at night. A local farmer painted white stripes on his cows in case they strayed onto the roads.

21

Lowestoft's population was reduced by two-thirds when most of the children and many of the mums were evacuated. Some went to stay with relatives in safer inland towns and villages, but many children were sent to distant places and spent the years of the war with people they had never seen before.

On June 2 1940, 2,969 children left in five special trains. 'Danger of Invasion' posters were pasted up everywhere, and all people not needed for the running of the town were advised to leave for a safer place. Many refused to go, including, of course, our mum. But she did send brother Pud to stay with our Granny who ran a pub in rural Norfolk. He stuck it for a month or two, then sniffed out a fish lorry and got a lift back to Lowestoft fish market and a bus home.

'What on earth are you doing home?' said our Mum.

'I want to go fishing,' replied Pud.

'Well, that's that,' said Mum, 'if we are going to be blown up, we'll be blown up together.'

IMPORTANT NOTICE

EVACUATION

The public throughout the country generally are being told to " stay put " in the event of invasion. For military reasons, however, it will in the event of attack be necessary to remove from this town all except those persons who have been specially instructed to stay. An order for the compulsory evacuation of this town will be given when in the judgment of the Government it is necessary, and plans have been arranged to give effect to such an order when it is made.

You will wish to know how you can help NOW in these plans.

THOSE WHO ARE ENGAGED IN WORK OF ANY DESCRIPTION IN THE TOWN SHOULD STAY FOR THE PRESENT.

OTHER PERSONS SHOULD, SO FAR AS THEY ARE ABLE TO DO SO, MAKE ARRANGEMENTS TO LEAVE THE TOWN—PARTICULARLY

> MOTHERS WITH YOUNG CHILDREN
> SCHOOL CHILDREN
> AGED AND INFIRM PERSONS
> PERSONS WITHOUT OCCUPATION OR IN RETIREMENT.

All such persons who can arrange for their accommodation with relatives or friends in some other part of the country should do so. Assistance for railway fares and accommodation will be given to those who require it.

Advice and, where possible, assistance will be given to persons who desire to leave the town but are unable to make their own arrangements.

Information about these matters can be obtained from the local Council Offices.

(*Signed*) WILL SPENS,
Regional Commissioner for Civil Defence.

CAMBRIDGE,
    2nd July, 1940.

(393/4177) Wt. 19544-30 125M 7/40 H & S Ltd. **Gp. 393**

CHURCHMAN'S CIGARETTES

THE CIVILIAN RESPIRATOR—HOW TO ADJUST IT

CHURCHMAN'S CIGARETTES

THE CIVILIAN RESPIRATOR—HOW TO REMOVE IT

People gave up carrying masks after a few months. We were taught to spit on the inside of the mica window to prevent it misting up. Gas masks were good for rude noises and fogged up anyway.

Hitler will send no warning –
so always carry your gas mask

ISSUED BY THE MINISTRY OF HOME SECURITY

THE SHOP

Our mother ran the village shop. She sold everything, from sweets to sealing wax and string. The pavement outside was piled high with vegetables. Inside, the shop always seemed full of legs. Khaki legs, sailors' legs, busmen's legs and, worst of all, little old ladies' legs. I had a horror of being trapped under voluminous dark skirts smelling of rotten lavender and cats' pee.

Our home and shop stood with two other little houses on a kind of triangular traffic island surrounded by three roads. It was at the end of the bus route from town, and after turning the buses around, the drivers and conductors had five minutes' break.

Mother made tea in a great big pot, and the busmen drank it from saucers as they couldn't wait for it to cool.

The soldiers and sailors had more time. They stood about the shop and joked and told stories while they drank their tea, saucer in one hand, cup in the other and a ciggy smouldering between two fingers. Often they filled the shop and spilled out on to the pavement. Ordinary customers, old men coming for their tobacco and old ladies doing their bits of shopping, had to push their way through the throng. Younger ladies didn't seem to mind the crush and enjoyed the jokes I didn't understand.

All the young local men were away, in uniforms, drinking tea and getting shot at some place else.

One day, the scream of a falling bomb sent everyone in the shop diving into a heap on the floor. Tea everywhere. The house of Mr Lang, the chemist just up the road, was destroyed.

We had no garden. The tiny yard at the back was filled with sacks of potatoes, carrots and turnips. Even our big tin bath on the coal bunker was full of cabbages and cauliflowers from one Saturday bath night to the next.

The shop, then, was the playground of my toddler years. That the shop was perpetually full of soldiers and sailors seemed quite normal to me. In 1940 the whole world seemed full of soldiers and sailors. It was fun crawling in and out of their legs, while they stood among the sacks of veg and drank tea and joked. It was educational too. I learned very colourful language. This I directed at any approaching old lady's legs.

The men decided this child needed discipline. I was drilled every morning. Dressed either as a soldier or sailor, depending on who was to be Drill Sergeant, I was inspected in the shop, then marched up and down the pavement while massed ranks of tea drinkers shouted, 'Left Right, Left Right, About Turn, Pick Them Feet Up!'

Our loo was in the back yard, and there was a bus stop next to the wall of the loo. The Number 4 bus arrived at that stop every thirty minutes, but the queue of people started forming long before the bus was due. I hated going to the loo with a queue of locals chatting just the other side of the wall, especially if I thought I was going to be noisy (during the pea season for instance). I used to try to time it so that I was doing my business just as the engine of the bus was thundering away and the conductor was shouting, 'Move along inside, please.'

More than sixty thousand sailors moved into Lowestoft as the naval base grew. The base was sited in a little wooded park called Sparrow's Nest. All it had was a small concert hall, a thatched cottage, an open-air bandstand and a goldfish pond. There were no barracks, so all the sailors had to be accommodated in boarding houses and any spare rooms around the district. The town was choked with sailors, in fact they were told to walk along the sea front rather than block the main street. Adding to the congestion were the thousands of soldiers who did their final assault training along the cliffs before going overseas. As well as the British troops there were Free French, Poles and Czechs. Almost every household had uniformed lodgers.

Thousands of sailors strolling along the sea front was too good a target to miss, and there were many dive bomber raids.

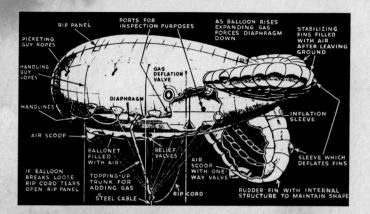

RIP PANEL
PORTS FOR INSPECTION PURPOSES
AS BALLOON RISES EXPANDING GAS FORCES DIAPHRAGM DOWN
STABILIZING FINS FILLED WITH AIR AFTER LEAVING GROUND
PICKETING GUY ROPES
HANDLING GUY ROPES
GAS DEFLATION VALVE
HANDLINES
DIAPHRAGM
INFLATION SLEEVE
AIR SCOOP
BALLONET FILLED WITH AIR
RELIEF VALVES
AIR SCOOP WITH ONE-WAY VALVE
SLEEVE WHICH DEFLATES FINS
IF BALLOON BREAKS LOOSE RIP CORD TEARS OPEN RIP PANEL
TOPPING-UP TRUNK FOR ADDING GAS
RIP CORD
RUDDER FIN WITH INTERNAL STRUCTURE TO MAINTAIN SHAPE
STEEL CABLE

The arrival of barrage balloons had all the excitement of the arrival of the circus big top.

The extra member of our household was Aunt Louie. Her husband died about the same time as my father. She came to help my mother and was a powerful force around the place. She did everything with gusto. Her laughter stopped traffic.

On Mondays the scullery would be full of steaming washing, with the huge copper boiling away, Aunt Louie winding the wheel of the old mangle, and the bleached wooden rollers spurting rainbows through clouds of steam.

The scullery was also where the teas were made, so mother was back and forth through this pandemonium with cups and saucers. The big black kettle added its puffs to the huffing and puffing of Aunt Louie as she sang along to the radio. It was like living in a very active volcano.

Mum and Aunt Louie were a good team. They had a wonderful way with the legions of men who, for a brief moment in the tumult of their lives, found a cup of tea, a cigarette and a chat at the corner shop.

Some stayed longer. Some formed friendships which continue still. But for many of them our substitute family was to be the last family they would know.

Even today Aunt Louie cries when she talks about 'all those lovely boys'. And then, drying her eyes, she says, 'Oh, but we had the time of our lives.' Certainly the air was rich with jokes and banter, no doubt bawdy much of the time. It would come rippling up the stairs as I slipped into sleep.

Wash Day (Painted 1951)

The long, the short and the tall engaged in endless card games. Len, tall, thin and ginger; Darkie, Lofty, Dusty, Pop; and Adam, killed in Burma aged just nineteen.

One particular friend of Mum and Aunt Louie was a big sailor from Mevagissy called Pop. He used to fill my head with tales of Cornwall, a land full of smugglers and seas full of shipwrecks.

One day, Pop took me out for the day to Beccles. We rowed about on the river, and he showed me how to put a worm on a hook and then I fell in. It would have been against naval regulations for Pop to part with any of his uniform, so I rode home on the bus in his giant vest.

Worse was to follow. A few days later, 'Aunt Tishie' (like many of my Aunts, she was not even remotely related) took me to her house for dinner and a run in the fields.

Sitting at the dinner table I was too shy to ask to go to the loo – and pooed in my pants. When her nose told her what had happened she washed me down in the copper and dressed me in a pair of enormous bloomers. She then marched me home and into the shop, past massed ranks of tea drinkers, to a chorus of 'Left Right, Left Right!' and 'Wot uniform do you call that, Sergeant Major?'

There was no shortage of uniformed knees to sit on in the evenings. Soldiers and sailors were billeted in most of the houses round about, and my Mum's front room was a favourite place for a card school. They sat round the table under a cloud of smoke. They couldn't get their knees under the table because, of course, that space was occupied by boxes of powdered milk, as were all corners of the room.

They loved to come to parties. At one of my birthday parties, Gus the sergeant had fallen asleep on the settee with a cigarette in his hand. All the children sat and watched as the butt burned down to the flesh.

Christmas night, 1942, I remember looking back into the room as Mother carried me to the stairs. A sea of faces in the smoke. They were dressed as soldiers and sailors but wearing paper hats. Other boys' fathers, sitting round our table wishing it was their little boy they had just kissed goodnight.

A village shop window, stuffed full, with nothing costing more than a penny (you could ask for a penn'orth of anything) is a sight no child can pass. The children of Pakefield were poor. A penny to spend was a rare treat. The spending required a lot of thought and took a lot of time. The penny was spent many times over in the imagination as they peered over the boxes of veg outside the shop at the rows of glass jars at the back of the window.

Pear drops, humbugs, fruit drops, liquorice comforts, gob-stoppers. You got more pear drops for a penny, but you might have to share them with your little brother or sister, or any of the notorious *Botwright* brothers if you happened to meet one in a back opening. Gob-stoppers last longer and you were less likely to have to share (although half-sucked gob-stoppers were often passed round, usually from my pocket and then mouth to mouth through the Botwright hierarchy).

Liquorice comforts were most fun. They were sucked slowly until only the black centre remained. This stained all your teeth black. If you were careful you could blacken only a few, or every other one. Earlier in the sucking stage, while there was still colour on the comforts, you could war-paint yourself and several other members of the gang in the full range of candy colours. Psychedelia came early to the Hill Green Gang.

Now, it was my good fortune, as a toddler, to be placed in the middle of this Aladdin's Cave of penny treasures. The only place safe from the feet of busmen and the Allies, and where my mother could keep an eye on me, was in the shop window. Also, away from the dark threat of their skirts, I was less likely to be rude to old ladies.

This was my window on the world. A window criss-crossed with anti-blast sticky tape, but a window which burnt penny-sized holes in the pockets of children in the street. A window past which swirled the machinery of war, the baker's horse-drawn van, the brewers' drays, and Stewey White, the tipsy coalman whose horse took him home every night.

Every ten minutes or so a bus crew would arrive for their five-minute tea break. They liked it 'hot 'n' strong'.

At one end of the glass counter was a big wooden bakers' tray, full of very dull-looking cakes. Some had a fingerprint of jam on top to suggest memories of a cherry. Others had a little black currant on top. If you saw a cake with two currants, one of them would be a fly.

Sitting in the shop window in summer was not without danger. Any bruised fruit attracted swarms of wasps. The wasps would gorge themselves for a while, then climb with sticky feet part way up the window and doze off in the sun. Boys outside the window would pretend to lick them off, or drum on the glass with their fingers and stir the wasps up into such a fury that they would dive-bomb the closely packed tea-swilling customers.

I don't think I was ever stung, despite having the stickiest face and fingers in the village.

THE K.O.S.B.'S

The King's Own Scottish Borderers manned positions around the district, and Company D was billeted in Pakefield School and a large cottage next door called Rookery Nook. Many were in tents in the garden.

The men of Company D were a particularly friendly lot, and Gus Dalgliesh had a miniature uniform made for me. I was inspected each morning in the shop, and any dullness of button or smudge of chalk on the chequered capband was duly noted. Apparently I took all this very seriously, and was particularly spick and span each time Company D marched past on church parade.

On one occasion a crowd of King's Own Scottish Borderers were in the bar of the Tramway pub, opposite our shop, when a pack of raiders suddenly dived and machine-gunned the street. The KOSBs and other customers hit the floor, and the only casualties were two or three pints on the mantelpiece above the fire. Two other KOSB lads were less fortunate. They were taking a dixie of tea around to comrades in the positions when the raiders attacked. They dropped the tea and dived for cover. They landed head first in a pigsty owned by an old character known as 'Pigmalion'. They were not warmly welcomed when they finally arrived with the tea.

Talking of smells, the soldiers used to raid the nearby pea fields when they felt hungry. They would eat their fill, then stuff their kitbags to share with their mates. Queer noises were heard through the night, caused by what they called 'musical fruit'.

but we were all sorry to leave Pakefield and its people, it was home from home. it was very early in the morning when we left it was dark when the army trucks moved out to an unknown destination. every lad said their good-byes earlier and there was some tears shed more so in the wee shop. and as we moved past your abode. the light was shining a fond farewell. and I kept my promise.

Following the departure of the KOSBs came the 6th Battalion of the King's Regiment, comprised mostly, it seemed, of Liverpool Irish. One of them gave a deafening performance on his bagpipes in our front room.

THE HILL GREEN GANG

As I got older, my world stretched along the London road to Hill Green. Why it was called Hill Green is a mystery. It was just the opposite. It was a hole in the ground, an old gravel pit.

At the bottom of the pit squatted the communal air-raid shelter. This was a huge square grassy mound, with air vents on top, and a flight of concrete steps descending into the dark mouth. A chilling place, frequently swilling with water, the wooden duck-boards bobbing about like life-rafts.

Local families, those without their own shelters, or who felt safer under the thick covering of concrete and earth, descended the steps in the evening, bringing their bedding in prams and wheelbarrows. Elderly people, particularly those living on their own, liked the company, and perhaps felt there was safety in numbers.

I never went there at night. We had our trusty Anderson and Morrison shelters, and the pantry under the stairs where Pud and Ivan slept.

In the daytime, the Hill Green shelter became our favourite place to play. Its grassy slopes, covered in spring and summer with wild flowers, were Wild West mountains from which we could swoop down on to the plains and attack Brenda Smith and the other 'settlers' playing 'house' in the abandoned Builders' Yard.

Most of my friends lived in the roads bordering Hill Green. It was our territory. Children from other districts strayed there at their peril.

Once we caught the leader of the Ship Road Gang, who was called 'Woof'. He was tied to a ladder and smoked over a damp fire on the steps of the shelter. I don't remember if Woof was supposed to be a German or a Cowboy.

For some reason, we always liked to be the Indians. Cowboys were so clean and broke into songs and yodels. Also, we wanted to be the pirates, the smugglers, the highwaymen, the cut-throats every time, and never the 'goodies'.

Of course we played 'British and Germans' from time to time, but no one would 'be' the Germans, so we couldn't indulge in the hand-to-hand grappling that we enjoyed. We had to be satisfied with long-range sniping at imaginary foes or a passing old lady. 'Dive bombing', with arms outspread, thumbs firing and engine screaming, was a favourite with us and very unpopular with old ladies. But none of us would ever 'be' the Germans.

The Hill Green shelter was also used in the real war for manoeuvres. A position to be surrounded, scaled and taken by wave after wave of soldiers in training. From a trench next to the little field where the baker kept his van horse, the troops crept in various formations towards the 'enemy stronghold'. Sometimes there were thunder flashes and smoke bombs to add to the drama.

At other times, motorcycle dispatch riders (male and female) came there for training, and careered up and down the slopes, wheels spinning and mud flying. I remember one bike bouncing down the slope and bursting into flames.

Motorcycle side-car combinations, with a gun mounted on the side-car, also roared and slithered over our Hill Green.

They would come and go, the soldiers. This battalion, that battalion. We knew all their badges and where they were from. But we, like them, never knew where they were going.

RAIDERS

Because of the nearness of the town to enemy airfields, usually there was no warning of attack – just a roaring engine from low cloud, a couple of loud 'crumps' and a hail of machine-gun fire. It was all over in seconds. Then, as the dust began to settle and the raider was escaping back over the North Sea, the warning wail of the siren would begin. This could be repeated several times in a day, or there might be a lull for a week or more.

Rainy, misty mornings were the times of greatest fear. Lowestoft's worst raid was on a day of snow, just before dusk. One lone raider loomed out of cloud above the main street and dropped four bombs on to shops and a crowded restaurant.

Seventy people were killed and more than a hundred injured. The individual dive-bomber made it seem much more personal – one enemy plane looking for someone to kill.

Opposite the Green was the Fire Station. Exhausted fire crews, sitting on the gleaming red engines, watched the war games on the Green.

Some London firemen were sent to Lowestoft for a rest from the Blitz. They found the frequent, unpredictable hit-and-run raids of the east coast even more exhausting.

The first alarm was sounded at 11.02 a.m. on the first day of the war, Sunday, 3 September 1939; the last on Monday, 30 April 1945. The 'alert' was sounded 2,047 times, with 112 warnings in August 1940 alone.

One afternoon we children were mucking about with a football on the recreation ground, or 'Rec', as we called it. Jack, the oldest of the Botwright brothers, shouted 'Fokkers!' We ran like rabbits for the slip trenches under the trees. Twelve Fokker Wulfes swooped out of the sky without warning and flew the whole length of the town spraying cannon shells. They dropped their bombs at the north end. The back of our house was riddled with cannon fire.

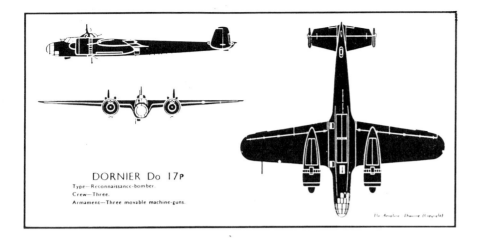

DORNIER Do 17P

Type—Reconnaissance-bomber.
Crew—Three.
Armament—Three movable machine-guns.

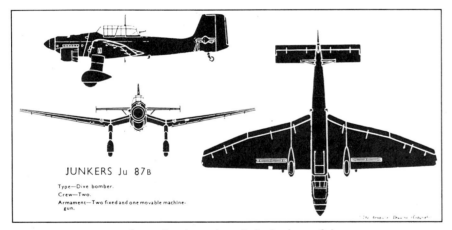

JUNKERS Ju 87B

Type—Dive bomber.
Crew—Two.
Armament—Two fixed and one movable machine-
gun.

As well as knowing all the badges of the army, we children knew all the shapes and sounds of aircraft. Especially enemy aircraft. Although the fields and woods teamed with butterflies and birds, our skies and minds were full of planes.

At night Dorniers, Heinkels and Junkers, in packs of hundreds, droned over our heads for the industrial heart of the Midlands. But they did not all pass over. Sometimes one or two planes, perhaps with sick engines, dumped their load on the first town they reached.

The Borough Surveyor said in 1944 that 125 per cent of houses in the area had been either damaged or destroyed. This meant that some were damaged twice and some three times.

There were narrow escapes. Brother Pud arrived home early from school one day to say it had been bombed. A lone enemy aircraft had swooped down, almost hitting the school, climbed and circled and dropped three high explosive bombs. It was a sunny lunchtime, and Pud and his friends were playing by a corrugated iron fence in the playground. Although blown down by the bomb, the fence deflected enough of the blast to save the children. The school was wrecked. No one was seriously injured at the school, but people were killed elsewhere in the village.

Two hundred bombs dropped in fields nearby, and a partridge died of shock. A high explosive bomb fell on a garden plot and blew away a chicken house. A nearby chicken house was left with only one wall standing, but the birds were found sitting on their usual perches.

Friends struggled from their shelter to find their home a pile of bricks, but managed to rescue their canary, still singing in its battered cage.

One result of the bombing was that millions of seeds would be blown out of gardens and showered around the district. The following spring and summer, piles of rubble burst into bloom. Marigolds, irises and, best of all, potatoes sprouted everywhere.

FRIENDS AND LOCALS

One of my boyhood friends was aptly named 'Squirt'. He was small and the son of a fireman. He had a fireman's axe, the next best thing to a tomahawk. Another friend was 'Wimps'. Although a member of the Ship Road gang, he was admired for eating horse dung, in the road, for a bet.

The main London Road ran along one side of the Green and was very busy, both with local traffic and the traffic of war. But the two small roads forming the other two sides of the Green were virtually unused by motor traffic, and only the occasional bike interrupted our games of street football. We played a kind of street tennis with our feet. Sometimes passing sailors or off-duty soldiers would join in and it would be several minutes before we got our ball back.

One of the small side roads trailed off into an unpaved lane full of dips and puddles known as 'the Bumps'. It divided Hill Green from a small dense wood and was the scene of many an ambush and highway robbery.

Our trails criss-crossed the landscape of childhood. We galloped Indian file through sage brush and tumble weed, one hand holding an invisible rein and the other slapping the seat of our trousers.

Front doors were rarely opened, except to scrub the front step. The bike was out the back, and the back openings – the narrow lanes between the back-to-back houses – were the main thoroughfares. Nobody I knew had a car. We had no car, but we did have a piano as an ornament and a camera with no film.

Each back opening was lined with tremendously high 'linen posts' carrying the clothes lines. They were as high as ships' masts. They *were* ships' masts, with ships on top. The little fleet sailed the high seas above the billowing laundry. The sheds in the back yards were where we played on rainy days. Brenda Smith and the girls were always trying to put on back-yard musicals.

A billy-goat escaped during an air raid, and we chased it into our maze of back openings. It then decided to chase *us* – in and out of backyards, biting chunks out of the hanging washing. It eventually cornered Kenny and started eating his hair. Various mums with brooms rescued Kenny and we drove the goat into the field where the fishing nets were tanned and hung out to dry. The goat was then netted as if he were a tiger. By the time the farmer arrived, his goat had eaten his way out of the net but, appetite aroused, had started on a whole line of drying nets.

Of course, living in the shop, I was luckier than my friends when it came to treats. I didn't need a penny, and I didn't need to press my nose to the outside of the window and ponder the merits of sherbet lemons over barley sugar. As a toddler, I could help myself to a packet of sweet cigarettes and get a 'light' off a sailor. When I was a little older a sailor gave me a puff of a real cigarette, and I haven't tried a cigarette since.

From the age of about five, we used to smoke a weed called Tramps' Delight. It was a tall plant with thin curly leaves. When they had been dried, we rolled them in strips of newspaper, or stuffed them into home-made pipes fashioned from 'pipe wood' trees. Dried hawthorn leaves were plentiful but not so good.

From time to time we had the treat of a real tramp on our patch. They usually set up a little camp on the 'bumps' beside the wood. No doubt they were suspicious of us children, but we were usually granted an audience if we were respectful enough, and waited until invited to the fireside.

The tramp would tell us a few tall stories of the world. None of us children had been much further than the next village. Even the soldiers, the airmen and most of the young sailors, recently called up, had experience only of their home town or village. But a tramp, a 'King of the Road', could have been everywhere, and frequently told us he had. After bringing him bits of food from home, we watched and learned how to set up a fire safely, cook a pot of stew and spit with unerring accuracy on to the bobbing lid of the black boiling kettle.

Another teller of tall tales was an old fisherman we called Father Christmas because of his long white whiskers. He told tales of his cabin boy days on the great clippers and sailing ships.

On his first voyage he got homesick and jumped ship in Falmouth, the last stop before Rio. He hitched and worked his way through Cornwall and all the way home to Lowestoft. This was the first I had heard of Cornwall. He described it as a land of rocks and shipwrecks. Later, 'Pop' the sailor would tell me more. But I was already hooked.

Now, every time I drive over desolate Bodmin Moor towards my studio at St Ives, I think of the cabin boy hitching home to Suffolk.

Brother Pud, although still a schoolboy, was a very keen fisherman, and one of the old longshoremen, Alan Page or 'Pagey', took him under his wing and taught him all he knew.

'Pagey' developed a special understanding with the Commanding Officer of the large Czech Force stationed along the cliff, and eventually the longshore fishermen were allowed to venture through a secret gap in the defences and fish. They needed special permits and had to inform the authorities if they intended fishing after dark. Occasionally some would be arrested for getting back late after being unable to resist one more haul in the fading light.

'Pagey' and the Czech Commander were an incongruous couple but saluted one another with obvious respect. 'Pagey' used his rowing boat to tow and position the target for the long-range guns inland at Mutford. Thanks to his knowledge of tide and current, and spotters on the cliff top radioing range and trajectory, the gunners lobbed shells over the fields and villages to land more or less on target offshore.

The Czechs were particularly keen on fishing and were happy to help with hauling boats and cleaning nets. When a seal was seen eating the cod off the fishermen's long lines, the army put two sharpshooters into Page's boat to shoot it.

Pud and the other fishermen were also granted extra rations of cheese for their sandwiches, as the fish they caught were a valued addition to the local diet. They also received extra clothing coupons for rubber boots.

Rubber boots were hard to come by, and used to be heavily patched. When a landing craft got into difficulties, all the men were taken off and it eventually ran aground along Pakefield beach. Billy Trip, out fishing at the time, was first aboard the stricken vessel and, local hero that he was, pinched a pair of wellies. When he got them home he found they were both left feet.

On another occasion 'Pagey' found a stray mine on the shore. He put it in his wheelbarrow and took it to the Police Station. It could have blown up half of Pakefield.

'Father Time' was another old character around the village. A veteran of the First World war, he was a rather elderly Special Constable during the Second. He was suspicious of the telephone, and usually asked our mother to make his reports from the public phone box on 'the corner'. He helped in the shop from time to time, humping sacks of potatoes from the back yard to the front, and telling the troops they didn't know what a 'real' war was.

Another character who was always popping into the shop was Sid, the man from the Co-op who bought warts. He bought mine for sixpence. He gave me sixpence and my warts disappeared. He had a clubfoot. I imagined his boot full of all the warts of the village.

THE YANKS ARE COMING

Late in 1942 the traffic past our shop began to include
trucks and jeeps of the USAAF. We used to run behind
the trucks full of waving men and shout 'Got any gum
chum?' We were usually showered with packets of
chewing gum and biscuits.

They spoke like heroes. They all sounded like cowboys.
(In fact, James Stewart was a flyer at a nearby base.) I
dreamed that if I ran behind enough trucks they would
spot me as the new Mickey Rooney and we would all go
to Hollywood.

Hundreds of huge Flying Fortresses and Liberators would
leave their bases in the farmlands behind Lowestoft and
fill the sky like a giant iron net and thunder off toward
Germany. When they came back there would be many
gaps in the net. Some would return late and low, badly
shot up and trying to keep out of the icy sea.

In the evenings they were determined to enjoy themselves. Some of my friends had big sisters, so they got to know the Yanks well.

From trees outside the Lowestoft Palais de Dance we could watch them jitterbugging, and sing along with the crooner. I decided to play a trumpet in a swing band instead of going to Hollywood.

SCHOOLDAYS

Around 1942 the local school was re-opened. The male teachers were all away in the war, so we were taught by ladies, many of them elderly. The only man in the school was the Headmaster. His wife taught the top class, and the big boys told us little ones horror stories of the punishments she gave them.

The oldest teacher was Miss West, who, we all thought, must be at least a hundred. She taught the youngest children. She was tiny and dressed from top to bottom in grey and lavender. I should say top to toe, because when she swung herself up on to her high stool we got a glimpse of her long drawers, held by elastic below the knee. Sometimes they were a startling periwinkle blue.

Eventually, she noticed our interest and, occasionally, would hoist her hem demurely and say, 'The colour today, children, is blue' (or bottle green or whatever). Then she swung herself up on to her stool and the day would begin.

Apart from the Headmaster and his horror wife, the teachers were kind. However, Miss Burgess was provoked into mass punishments when she returned to

the classroom to find us goose-stepping around and doing the Nazi salute.

'How dare you! How dare you when your fathers are away fighting Hitler!'

It was the usual wooden ruler on the palm of the hand. Probably just two strokes apiece.

There were many alarms. Some false, some real and some late.

Just the threat of being sent to the Headmaster was usually sufficient to stop us getting out of hand, but towards the end of the war, a dozen of us were finally sent to his office.

We had decided to help a squad of Italian prisoners of war demolish and move the rubble of our old air-raid shelters. We used some of the bricks to bomb litter baskets hung around the walls of the playground – and caused more damage than the Luftwaffe.

We were kept quaking in the corridor for ages until all the other children had gone home. We were sure to be taken down to his wife's torture chamber. What actually happened, I don't remember. Perhaps it was so horrific I have blotted it from my memory. But probably it was just the old ruler again.

For years afterwards, when I delivered Sunday papers to the Headmaster and his wife, I would try to float silently over their crunching gravel . . . and a chill would come from their letter-box.

As the war dragged on, prisoners of war became a familiar sight and were a useful force on the farms. The Italians in particular were always ready for a game of football. Some married local girls. Our cousin Gwen married a German P.O.W. (After the war they came on a visit in a Messerschmitt bubble car.)

LIFE'S EARLY DISAPPOINTMENTS

My favourite delivery man was Charlie McCarthy with his fruit and veg truck. Toward the end of the war, as more convoys of ships got through, the fruit in Charlie's truck became more exotic. An occasional barrel of grapes packed in cork chippings was like a lucky dip. I liked to dig my fingers down through the cork and pull out big bunches of grapes smelling of overseas.

Then, at last, came the great day when the first long banana box was slid from the truck on to Charlie's shoulders, and into the shop. A space was hurriedly cleared on the floor. The lid, which must have been about five feet long, was prised off with a claw hammer. But inside, instead of the five foot long banana I expected, were rows of little yellow hands with green fingertips.

72

It was an anti-climax equalled only by my first visit to the pictures. When the threat of air raids was thought to be over, Pop, the sailor, took me to the Odeon. We went to see John Wayne in *Stage Coach*. Sitting in the dark was thrilling. At the far end of the darkness was Mexico, all orange and yellow, a flight of white steps with deep blue shadows leading to an arch with red roof tiles. There was green cactus and a volcano in the background.
I waited for John Wayne to gallop down the steps.

A man played a few rousing tunes on the organ, then the blazing colours of Mexico disappeared slowly up into the darkness to reveal a little flickering black-and-white screen behind. All the movement and noise and Indians couldn't make up for the lost promise of Mexico. The best bit of the film was the strange curly black hair that twirled and vibrated in the corner of every scene. Sometimes it suddenly uncurled and lashed across the screen like a serpent.

73

FARM DAYS

An old single-decker bus took us over the Dam and
across the marshes. We got off the bus at the rise of the
hill, before the beech wood. The Ruthern's cottage on
the farm's land stood in the shade of a giant pear tree. In
front of the cottage was the old well, smelling of mossy
brick and deep cool water.

From there, the land sloped to the water meadows
and marshes and on eventually to the grey sea. Always
grey, even in high summer, This low land was criss-
crossed with dikes, thick with bullrushes and alive with
sticklebacks and dragonflies.

Great variety of grasses. Some perfect for picking your teeth, some for whistles, some for making rude noises, some for darts, and some for looping into a noose which, when pulled tight, catapults the head of the grass like a cannon ball. The white trumpets of bindweed were great for catching bees.

All seen close-up as we slithered commando-style, faces camouflaged with mud, bullrush bayonets bristling at the end of their green barrels.

We were savages, chasing rabbits with knobbly sticks.
Their last refuge was the dwindling rectangle of standing
corn — a golden citadel about to fall.

us, the grown 'slow' man and me, aged six, used to spend hours chasing Germans in a jeep with no wheels.

At the end of a day a special pleasure was hauling water from the well. A whirl of the iron handle sent the bucket hurtling down to strike the water like a dead bell. It would sink with a couple of lurches. Then the struggle of winding it up, the bucket swinging slowly dropping diamonds in the dark.

Then into the cottage for Mrs Ruthern's rabbit pie. The crust thick and golden and dark brown round the edges. Steam poured from the white funnel in the centre, and more steam when the knife went in, and the smell of carrots and onions. The first big triangle went to Mr Ruthern's plate with a mountain of potatoes from the garden. There was milk from the cows, water from the well. Everything else came from the garden. Currants and gooseberries, and delicious cooking apples. Pears hard as flint, and small, soft yellow ones. All kinds of plums and greengages and strange and wonderful varieties of apple.

Mr Ruthern cut the bruises off the windfalls with his clasp knife and ate the slices off the blade. From time to time he would stretch over the table toward me and I loved to take the slice from the blade. His hand and forearm were nut brown, but when he stretched and his sleeve slid up, his arm was startlingly white.

After the meal he would make sure his old gun was clean and put it away high out of reach, then doze off, his feet on a sleeping dog.

One time, a girl named Hazel stayed at the farm. We called her Hy Hazel after the actress. She was a bit posh and used to lean out of her bedroom window brushing her hair like Rapunzel and teasing us boys.

I remember taking her down through the beech wood to meet the old couple who lived in a little cottage with their grown-up son. The son was a bit 'slow' but wonderful with birds and animals.

The Americans gave him a real jeep without wheels. They parked it outside his gate by the road. The two of

A RELIGIOUS EXPERIENCE

First day at Sunday school, six years old. Eight-year-old John Moore arrives red with excitement.

'You should see the apples,' he whispered. 'Millions of them. Easy. Just down the lane from here. Get over the fence easy.'

Tom and Billy Botwright, eyes shining, nod.

'Yeh, on our way home.'

The hot sunny afternoon, the droning vicar, the little pictures we were given to look at, the Lord's Prayer, full of words I didn't know the meaning of, and all the time my head full of apples and fences and fear.

Billy Botwright was my classmate, and tough, and I valued his friendship. I would do anything not to appear chicken in his eyes. Anything he would do, I would do.

The fence was bigger than I expected, and I couldn't see any apples at first. John Moore pointed out a few shrivelled little green ones at the tops of high branches. (My mother had a shop full of apples. Why was I trying to pinch these?) Around the trees was a quagmire liberally covered with chicken droppings. The chickens were as ominous as vultures.

Billy Botwright was first over the gate. We followed in a heap. By the time we reached the trees our boots were covered in so much slippery goo that climbing the trees was impossible.

Suddenly, the sunny Sunday afternoon was blotted out by a shape all black and Dracula. The Vengeance of the Lord – the Vicar defending his shrivelled cookers – had me by the throat.

The Botwrights had disappeared. John Moore was dropping to freedom from the top of the fence.

'Come back,' yelled the Vicar, Strather Hunt, 'I know who you are.'

'No fear!'

The Vicar pointed to a notice – Trespassers will be Prosecuted.

I was marched into the ghostly porch of the vicarage – not inside, because of the state of my boots.

'What's your name?' he asked through his fangs. I hoped there was a strong chain attached to his dog collar.

He knew who I was, so I told him.

'And who were the others?' Ah, my chance to be brave. Actually, I was too scared of Billy Botwright to ever tell on him.

The next day the village policeman, PC 'Pal' Whiteman arrived at our door. I hid under the front room table, and my mother said I was out. I heard PC Pal laugh and say something about 'as we forgive them who trespass against us'.

I should have paid more attention to the Lord's Prayer. So should have the Vicar.

DOODLEBUG!

The summer of 1944 saw the first 'doodlebugs'. Shaped like a plane but with no pilot, the doodlebug had a jet engine and fell to earth when the fuel ran out. They were aimed at London, but nine out of ten were shot down before they crossed the coast. Some were 'winged' and went off on an erratic course over the town. Local people flocked to the cliff-tops each evening to see the spectacular show as the doodlebugs came over the horizon to be met by the barrage of the coastal guns (now largely 'manned' by ATS girls). A direct hit would result in a tremendous orange flash, a bang and a shower of shrapnel, hopefully over the sea. But a 'winged' doodlebug could slide off in any direction. If its fiery tail went out it would hit the ground in fifteen seconds.

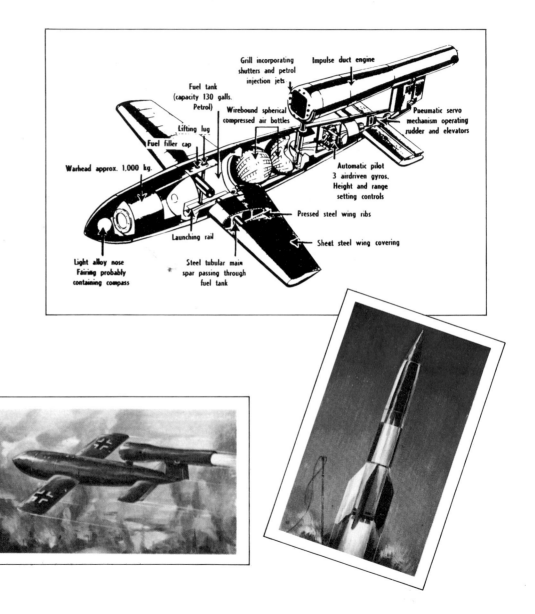

We were standing by our back door one evening watching a doodelbug drone overhead. Suddenly its red light went out. 'It's coming down!' someone yelled, and we rushed indoors and all dived under the Morrison shelter. I banged my head on the iron frame and forgot about the explosion.

It fell a mile away, on a farm. Next morning we all went to see the damage. The farm buildings were a pile of rubble and the air was full of feathers.

The doodlebug, or V1, was followed by the V2. They came silently, at any time, over the horizon, the deadly tip of a vapour trail a hundred miles long. Fired from deep within Europe as the Allies advanced. The east coast remained within range until the bitter end.

THE END

At the end of the war in Europe, 'Father Time' assumed responsibility for the bonfire celebrations. The accumulated junk and rubble of the war years made not one, but three huge heaps on Hill Green.

There was a competition for the best Hitler Guy, and there were some Himmlers, and Goebbels and many bald Mussolinis.

There has never been a Guy Fawkes night like it. All three bonfires went up together. All the Hitlers and henchmen toppled and blazed.

VJ Day was much the same. We burned Hitlers again, and a lot of yellow Guys with big teeth and glasses.

The big black-out blind from our front room window escaped the bonfires. My brothers made it into an enormous kite.

The windy day at the end of the war inspired many other kite makers. In my childhood, children's games seemed to come around in seasons. There was a time for hoops, a time for football, a time for fishing. This was the time for kites.

'It's too big. It won't fly!' shouted the boys as they held on to their kites and pushed and shoved to inspect mine. But it did fly. Such was the squabble to hold the line, however, that no one did.

It soared up over Hill Green and over the ashes of the victory bonfires, over the Fire Station and the road to London.

My eyes filled with pride and tears.

Toward the end of the day, Charlie McCarthy pulled up
outside the shop.

'What have you got for us today, Charlie?' asked Mum.

He grinned and hoisted me over his shoulder and
dumped me into the back of his truck. There, amongst
the fruit and veg, was my big black kite.

'It dive bombed me near the Dam' Charlie said.

So it was true, all the things the grown ups had said during the dark days. Now the war was over everything would be all right, there'll be blue birds over the white cliffs, not barrage balloons. And men with rainbows on their chests would, like my kite, come home.

And the memory of those who passed through our village on the way to war will remain for ever with the ghosts of us children in the fields and woods of long ago.

Received your letter with the very sad news of your
mother's passing, and with sadness in my heart her passing
has left me with a little emptiness. But I'm honoured to
have shared in her friendliness among so many, for so
many years. She was held in high esteem by her boys who
frequented the wee shop on the corner, for their sweets,
cigs, a coffee and a wee motherly chat – and when we
have our reunion this year we will remember her.

Gus Dalgliesh KOSB, May 1982